The Many Adventures of Peppy the Emperor Penguin

Short Stories, Fuzzy Animals, and Life Lessons

Norma MacDonald

Karma for Kids Books

The Many Adventures of Peppy the Emperor Penguin
Short Stories, Fuzzy Animals, and Life Lessons

Copyright © 2016 Norma MacDonald

First Edition

Published by: Find Your Way Publishing, Inc.
PO BOX 667
Norway, ME 04268 U.S.A.
www.findyourwaypublishing.com

ISBN-13: 978-1-945290-02-2

ISBN-10: 1-945290-02-1

Library of Congress Control Number: 2016940737

Printed in the United States of America.

Dedication

This book is dedicated to all of the people trying to make the world a better place. You are making a positive difference!

"How far that little candle throws his beams! So shines a good deed in a weary world." ~ *William Shakespeare*

Table of Contents

About This Book

Welcome to our Karma for Kids Books Series. We are very grateful that you picked up this book. We believe together we can make a positive difference, one child at a time. We strive to instill important life lessons in the lives of young children. We are firm believers in Karma and think that if this simple Law of the Universe is taught to children at a young age, their lives will have the potential to be absolutely amazing.

We once knew a dog named Karma. She was a beautiful, yellow Labrador retriever. It wasn't until after she passed, at 11 years old (God bless her loyal soul.), that we realized just how fitting her name really was.

Karma is indeed a retriever.

Whatever we threw out, Karma was always happy to bring it back to us. It didn't matter what it was, she always brought it back. If we threw out garbage, she'd bring it back without question. If we threw out the most beautiful dog toy, she'd bring it back. It's the same in life. Whatever you send out, is what you will get back. Guaranteed. Every time. Our Karma for Kids Book Series hopes to instill this easy-to-understand Law of the Universe into the lives of children at a young age. The Universe wants to happily bring you all that your heart desires, and it will, effortlessly. But first, you've got to throw out what you want it to bring back to you so that it can! Have fun with this and watch the magic happen. God bless!

Find all of Norma MacDonald's Karma for Kids Books at Amazon.com.

For more of our Karma for Kids books please visit us at:

www.karmaforkidsbooks.wordpress.com
or
www.findyourwaypublishing.com

Other books that we recommend to help children learn important life lessons:

Lucy Llama and Friends: Short Stories, Fuzzy Animals, and Life Lessons by Norma MacDonald

Ethan Eagle and Friends: Short Stories, Fuzzy Animals, and Life Lessons by Norma MacDonald

Billy Brown Bear and Friends: Short Stories, Fuzzy Animals, and Life Lessons by Norma MacDonald

Humble Heron and Friends: Short Stories, Fuzzy Animals, and Life Lessons by Norma MacDonald

Peter Penguin and Friends: Short Stories, Fuzzy Animals and Life Lessons by Norma MacDonald

Guaranteed Success for Kindergarten; 50 Easy Things You Can Do Today! by Marrae Kimball

Guaranteed Success for Grade School; 50 Easy Things You Can Do Today! by Marrae Kimball

The Secret Combination to Middle School: Real Advice from Real Kids, Ideas for Success, and Much More! by Marrae Kimball

Thank you!

The Many Adventures of Peppy the Emperor Penguin

Short Stories, Fuzzy Animals, and Life Lessons

Norma MacDonald

Karma for Kids Books

NORMA MACDONALD

Chapter One

Fair is Fair

IMAGINE WHAT IT WOULD be like if you lived inside a giant freezer. It's dark and very, very cold. Now imagine the wind is blowing inside that already cold freezer. But thankfully you are not alone. Many of your friends and family members are in that freezer with you. You cuddle up close together and share your warmth. You wait eagerly for the time to come when it won't be quite so chilly and dark.

This is what life is like for the Emperor Penguins living at the bottom of the earth on the cold, icy continent of Antarctica. This is the life of Peppy Penguin. She doesn't live in a freezer, but it feels like one. Thankfully she has lots and lots of waterproof feathers and a nice chubby layer of fat around her middle to help keep her warm. When she grows up she will be about the size of a six-year-old. But she's much littler now. Her white belly and black wings and head get bigger and bigger every day, but she's still smaller than all the grown up penguins around her.

But Peppy Penguin is much bigger than the itty bitty gray baby penguins that stick close to their parent's bellies. The babies don't have a gold stripe around their heads and necks like the bigger penguins. They're not old enough for that. Peppy Penguin is very proud of her yellowish gold stripes.

Peppy Penguin has many, many, many friends. She shares her icy cold home with lots of other types of penguins—large King penguins, medium-sized Adelie penguins, cute Chinstrap penguins, and itty bitty Gentoo penguins. She has a few friends who aren't penguins, like the big, big white bird called Albatross and the giant Elephant Seals. Some of the other animals aren't so friendly, like the Orcas. Penguins have to be very careful with the Orcas. They are called killer whales for a reason.

Antarctica is also home to many other birds and seals and whales. But mostly Peppy Penguin hangs out with other penguins. They help keep each other warm.

In the dead of winter, it is mostly dark day and night. The wind blows and it's cold, cold, cold. The only way for the penguins to survive is to stay huddled together. And even then, it's still so very, very cold. They don't have warm beds with cozy blankets to cuddle in. They have to stand outside in the cold.

This particular winter was darker and colder than any other winter the penguins had ever experienced. Peppy Penguin knew it wouldn't last forever, but many of her friends were not quite as patient. Proud Penguin and Pesky Penguin had been misbehaving, as usual. But before that story unfolds, let's learn a little bit more about how Peppy Penguin and her friends and family survive in their frozen, dark home.

The Emperor penguins have a special way of keeping warm called huddling. Peppy Penguin learned how to do this when she was very young. All of the penguins stand close together during a snowstorm and move around in a circle, spiraling towards the middle. Peppy Penguin remembers standing on her daddy's black furry feet so her own feet wouldn't get cold from standing on the ice. Her mommy and daddy took turns getting food for them to eat. One of them always stayed to keep her warm. All the young penguins cuddle up close to their parent's belly flap which is kind of like a warm blanket.

During the coldest part of the winter, all of the penguins stay close together and move slowly in a circle towards the middle of the huddle. The inside of the circle is where it's most warm. That's where all the penguins want to be. But the whole flock takes turns in the middle so that everyone gets the same amount of time in that safe warm place, surrounded by hundreds and hundreds of other penguins. Emperor penguins know about what's fair and what's not. Do you know what fairness is?

Have you ever seen someone cut in line? How did that make you feel? Did you think that wasn't fair?

Peppy Penguin stood with the large group of penguins between her mother and father, moving slowly toward the middle. There wasn't much to do, so she looked around to see if any of her friends were standing nearby so she could talk to them. That's when she saw Proud Penguin and Pesky Penguin step over and cut the line. They took one step and moved in front of at least 100 other penguins as they all moved toward the middle. But no one seemed to notice. Then she saw them do it again.

"Hey! That's not fair!" she said out loud.

"What's not fair?" asked her mom.

"Proud Penguin and Pesky Penguin just cut in line."

Peppy Penguin's dad cleared his throat. "That's a big accusation, my dear. Are you sure of what you saw?"

"I'm pretty sure," she said. "Are you gonna bust them, Daddy? I think you should tell on them."

Peppy Penguin's father chuckled and put his black wing around her. "I will look into it."

As he was talking, Peppy Penguin saw the two young penguins cut the line again. "Daddy. They just did it again!" she cried in a loud voice.

Many of the penguins turned their heads to see what she was talking about. Peppy Penguin pointed with her black wing. "They're cutting in line," she said, pointing to the two naughty penguins.

All the penguins around them started murmuring and muttering and asking questions. Who cut the line? Where are they? And what would be done about it? It had been a long time since anyone had tried to cut in line to get to the warmer center of the huddle. Would those naughty penguins be punished by being moved to the outside of the huddle where it was coldest? All the penguins waited to see what would happen. And they didn't have to wait long.

Peppy Penguin wasn't the only one who'd noticed the two penguins cutting the line. Two of the oldest penguins in the flock had also seen what they'd done. It wasn't long before Proud Penguin and Pesky Penguin were being lead to the outside of the huddle by the older penguins. They did indeed have to move to the outside of the huddle where it was coldest.

Peppy Penguin cuddled up closer to her parents. One of the things she loved about being a penguin was that everyone worked together to help keep each other warm in the winter. Everyone took turns as they moved toward the warm spot in the middle. Fair was fair. Cutting in line was not fair and although Peppy Penguin felt bad that they had to be moved to the outside of the huddle, she was happy that the two naughty penguins didn't get away with it.

As she moved slowly, step by step towards that warmer place in the center of the flock, Peppy Penguin thought about summertime and all the fun things she and her friends would do once the cold, dark winter ended. The freezing snow and wind blew around her head, but Peppy Penguin kept her thoughts focused on the future. Winter wouldn't last forever. She wondered how the naughty penguins were feeling and if they'd learned their lesson. She sure hoped so.

Chapter Two

The Baby Egg

PENGUINS ARE BIRDS. And when birds want to have children, they lay eggs, right? Having children in the freezing cold land of Antarctica is very, very difficult. Mama and papa penguins have to be extra careful to make sure their eggs are safe so that they will survive, hatch and become healthy, fluffy gray baby birds.

When Peppy Penguin learned that her mom had laid an egg and that she would have a little brother or sister, she was so very excited. The first time she saw the pear-shaped pale green egg she decided it would be a baby girl. Mostly because she really, really wanted a baby sister.

"When will I get to see her?" she asked. "Will she break out of the egg soon?"

"Be patient, my dear. It will take a couple of months before the egg hatches," her mother answered. "Now you need to get ready to come fishing with me. Your father will take good care of the egg."

"But can't I stay here with Papa and the egg?" Peppy Penguin asked. "I want to meet my baby sister as soon as she comes out."

"That's not a very good idea. There's nothing to eat here. You would get very, very hungry."

Peppy Penguin didn't give up. "But Papa won't have anything to eat either. What if something happens to him? Who will take care of the baby?"

"You shouldn't be worrying about that, my dear one. Nothing is going to happen to your Papa. He's a very strong penguin." Peppy Penguin's mama smiled and patted her on the head. "This isn't the first time he's taken care of an egg, you know."

Peppy Penguin still worried, though. The year before, her friend Patient Penguin's father wasn't able to take good care of his baby egg because he got too hungry and had to leave to go fishing. The baby egg never hatched. Peppy Penguin didn't want the same thing to happen to her baby sister.

"Mama, I really think I should stay with Papa. That way if he gets hungry I will be able to take care of the baby egg while he goes to get something to eat."

Peppy Penguin's mother felt good that her daughter was so faithful and wanted to stay, but she was concerned. "Let's go talk to your father about it," she said.

After much discussion amongst the three of them, it was decided Peppy Penguin could stay. Her mother waved a flipper-like black wing at her. "But it you start to get hungry, you will need to leave immediately and come directly to meet me at the ocean to catch fish. Do you understand?"

"I promise. I promise. I promise." Peppy Penguin jumped up and down with delight. She wouldn't have to leave the baby egg! She would be able to help her father and protect the egg from any dangers. And best of all, she would be there when the egg hatched and her new baby sister came out! She'd never seen an egg hatch before. She couldn't wait!

Peppy Penguin would be the best big sister ever. She would teach her baby sister everything she needed to know about living in Antarctica. She would help keep her warm in the winter. She would teach her how to slide on her belly across the ice. She would help her to learn how to hold her breath under water and how to catch lots and lots of fish and squid and the tiny little shrimp called krill.

But most importantly, she would teach her about the dangerous animals she would have to watch out for. Like the big birds, that grabbed little penguins--giant petrels and skuas. Then there was the huge problem of killer whales and leopard seals.

When Peppy Penguin was little, she almost got captured by one of the big black and white killer whales. Her father had grabbed her at the last second and pulled her to safety on the ice. She'd been so scared. She would definitely have to protect her little sister. She wouldn't let anything bad happen to her.

So for the next two months, Peppy Penguin faithfully and patiently stood next to her father, who kept the baby egg warm in his belly pouch. Both of them tried to ignore the growling and rumbling that came from their empty bellies. They didn't talk about food. But every day Peppy Penguin would ask him, "Is it time yet, Papa? Do you think she'll come out of the egg soon? Do you think today will be the day?"

Every day her father would answer her the same way. "She'll come out when she's ready to come out, little one. We must be patient. You can't rush these things."

As each day went by, they both got a little more hungry. The emptiness in Peppy Penguin's belly grew more and more painful. She didn't want to leave her father, but she was starting to think she should have gone with her mother to hunt for food. She thought about leaving her father and then returning before the baby egg hatched. But she was so afraid she'd miss it. She wasn't sure what to do. When the hunger pains in her belly got so bad that she didn't think she could stand another day, she decided to talk to her father about how she was feeling. "Papa, I don't want to miss baby girl hatching, but I don't know if I can go another day without food. Aren't you hungry? How can you stand it?"

Peppy Penguin's father sighed. "It is the sacrifice we fathers make because we love our children so much." He smiled and put a wing around her. "I made this same sacrifice for you, little one. And it was worth all the suffering."

"I never knew how difficult it was for papa penguins. I had no idea."

"And now you understand. I'm happy you have faithfully stayed with me all this time. I know you want to see the baby hatch, but I don't want you to put your life at risk. I think you need to go meet your mother and get that little belly of yours filled up."

Peppy Penguin's head dipped down to her chest. "I understand. But what if something happens to you? Who will take care of the baby egg?"

"I'll be fine, little one. When you and your mother return, your mother will feed me loads and loads of food. And your precious little sister will be waiting to meet you." He wrapped his wings around her. "Now you need to get going. Tell your mama everything is just fine here. Safe travels."

Reluctantly, Peppy Penguin started the long journey across the ice to the sea. She kept looking back and waving to her father until he was just a tiny black spot on the white horizon. She was weak and hungry, so the trip to the sea would take twice as long as normal. Her heart felt sad because she wouldn't be there to welcome her baby sister.

As Peppy Penguin slid across the ice the wind and cold struck her face. Everything was white, except for when she passed an occasional rock. The rocks were covered with red, orange, yellow or green stuff. Peppy Penguin thought they were very pretty.

On her way to the sea, she thought a lot about her parents. She felt a deeper love for them and had a new respect for both her mother and father. Emperor penguin parents in Antarctica have a very challenging and difficult life. Someday maybe she would have an egg of her own. She hoped that she would be a good mother. And she also hoped the father of her egg would be as faithful as her own.

Chapter Three

The Day Picky Penguin Wasn't So Picky Anymore

THE LONG DARK DAYS began to be a little brighter. It was the first sign that the hard days of winter were coming to an end. Peppy Penguin and her mother had returned to her father a few weeks earlier. Her beautiful little sister had indeed arrived. Her parents named her Peppy because she hatched out of the egg with lots and lots of energy. As soon as they got back, Peppy Penguin and her mother looked after the fuzzy baby bird and her father left to go fishing. All of the Emperor penguins would soon be moving to the coast together. It was summertime in Antarctica. The best time of the year.

When the Emperor penguins arrived at the coast, it was the happiest time for everyone. The chicks whistled in little groups together while their parents went fishing.

Peppy Penguin loved it when the flock moved to the coast. There was lots of fishing and swimming and playing and sunshine. No more cold, dark winter.

Peppy Penguin huddled with a group of her closest friends, Patient Penguin, Peppy Penguin, Pesky Penguin, Picky Penguin and Proud Penguin.

They'd been hanging out together since they were itty bitty fluffy babies. Picky Penguin only liked to eat squid and he hadn't been able to find any for three days already. Being fussy about what he ate seemed to make him really grumpy. All of his friends tried to get him to eat other things, but he always refused.

Most of the time, the young penguins fished as a group. They worked together to find schools of fish, squid, and krill. That morning they were about to dive into the place where they usually found squid when someone shouted. "Danger! Danger! Danger!"

All of them jumped away from the water just as a leopard seal emerged from the sea. No one was hurt, but now they couldn't go into the water until they knew that the leopard seals were gone. All of them were hungry, but none of them wanted to be lunch for the leopard seals.

"What are we gonna do now?" asked Pesky Penguin. "I'm hungry."

"We're all hungry," grumbled Picky Penguin.

"Let's just wait until it's safe," said Patient Penguin. "We can play a game or something."

So the group of young penguins decided to play their favorite game. They would see who could slide the furthest across the ice on their belly. Proud Penguin usually won. He was a great slider. But that day it was Picky Penguin who went the furthest. Unfortunately, he went too far. Way too far.

All the other penguins shouted at him as he slid quickly toward a large nanutak. "Watch out!"

But Picky Penguin thought they just didn't want him to win and before he knew it, he'd crashed into the big nunatak. Nunataks were the rock tippy tops of mountains. The rest of the mountains were buried under the ice. Picky Penguin hit his head on one of those rocks. All the other penguins hurried to see if he was okay. He was lying on his back with his eyes closed. "Is he dead?" asked Peppy Penguin, her face full of fear.

"I'm not dead," answered Picky Penguin, opening one eye. "But my head sure does hurt."

All the penguins huddled around him. "What can we do?"

His stomach grumbled. "I think I could eat an entire school of squid right now."

The other penguins all looked at each other. "Do you think it's safe to go back in the water yet?"

Pesky Penguin shook his head. "Why should we risk getting eaten just because Picky Penguin won't eat anything but squid?"

"If you were really hungry you would let us go get you some fish or krill."

Pesky Penguin shook his head, then groaned. "Ouch. My head hurts really bad."

"You need to rest," said Patient Penguin. "We'll see if we can find some squid somewhere else."

So they left Picky Penguin propped up against a rock and slid across the ice together toward the shore. They all hoped they could safely find a school of squid for him to eat. Before long, Peppy Penguin spotted her father and asked him if it was safe to go back in the water yet.

"Not here. You won't be able to get squid today, but there's plenty of krill and no danger if you go over there," her father said, pointing to the other side of the shore.

The group of penguins hurried over and dove into the water. All of them were hungry. They filled up their bellies until they couldn't take one more bite. Then they raced back to where they'd left Picky Penguin.

Now one thing that birds do, that humans would never do, is regurgitate their food. Regurgitate means that they spit their food back up and share it with each other. Humans would never do that, but penguins do it all the time. Mama penguins do it for their babies and for the papa penguins. Peppy Penguin and her friends would do it for Picky Penguin. But they didn't know if he was hungry enough to eat something other than squid.

They found Picky Penguin still propped up against the rocks. He didn't look good. "You're finally back. I'm so hungry I feel like I'm gonna pass out," he said. "Did you get me some squid?"

They all shook their heads. "No squid. Just krill."

Picky Penguin sighed. "I guess I'll just starve then."

"Come on," said Patient Penguin. "Can't you be reasonable? There's nothing wrong with krill and you need to eat *something*."

All of the other penguins nodded their heads in agreement. Picky Penguin's stomach growled. Everyone heard it. They all encouraged him to eat just a little. Just enough so that he'd have the energy to return to the flock. They all stood by waiting for his decision. Finally, he lowered his head and said,

"Go ahead and give me the krill. But I don't have to like it, right?"

All the penguins nodded, then they gave Picky Penguin loads of little shrimp to eat. At first, he made a sour face, but after a while, a smile washed over his face. "Hey," he said. "This isn't so bad after all."

From that day forward, Picky Penguin wasn't so picky anymore. He was willing to try new and different foods. No longer did he have grumpiness. At least not from hunger.

Chapter Four

Proud Penguin Didn't Think

ALL THE YOUNG PENGUINS liked to hunt food together. It was the safest and best way to hunt. From the time they were itty bitty fluffy gray penguins, their parents had warned them of the dangers from the seals and the killer whales. When they worked as a group, they could keep an eye out for the predators and protect each other. If they went off by themselves, they risked being captured.

All the young penguins knew about those dangerous animals. But sometimes, thinking they were being brave, one of the young penguins would get the idea that he or she could hunt alone. This was a very, very, very bad idea.

On this particular bright sunny day, Peppy Penguin and a group of about a dozen friends got up early in the morning to go hunting. Searching for schools of krill, fish, and squid with her closest friends always put a big smile on Peppy Penguin's face. As soon as the sun shone over the horizon, the small flock of young penguins met at the shore and one by one they dove into the ocean.

Darting underwater, they loved to play games together before the serious business of hunting food. Swimming under the waves gave Peppy Penguin a feeling of absolute freedom. Penguins were birds that couldn't fly, but when Peppy

Penguin was swimming underwater it felt like she was flying high in the sky. The penguins swooped and swirled and dove and spun around in circles. They played chase with one another, raced one another and of course, they hunted for food. But always, they kept alert to what was happening around them.

Proud Penguin played with the group for a bit of time, but after a little while, he got bored. He dove down deep under the water and had a look around. Off in the distance, he thought he spotted a large school of squid. But instead of telling his group of penguin friends, he decided he'd go fishing by himself. If he could encircle the school of squid and get them to change direction, he would be able to move the large group of squid closer to the shore and everyone would see what a great hunter he was.

As Proud Penguin chased after the school of squid, he imagined all the fluffy gray baby penguins standing on the icy shore clapping their wings and cheering and whistling for him. "Hooray! Hooray! Hooray!" they would shout. And then all the grown-up penguins would nod their heads and tell each other what a super fisherman he was.

Proud Penguin was so caught up in his dreams of greatness, he didn't notice the pair of large black and white whales who had begun to follow him. He had his eye on the school of squid and forgot to check the water around him like he'd been taught to do. In the meantime, the killer whales got closer and closer.

"I'll just dive down under the large swarm of squid and then swim to the back of the school and get behind them and chase them toward the shore,"

Proud Penguin said to himself as he glided quickly through the cold water. As he dove down, he thought he saw a dark shadow to his right and another to his left. Suddenly his heart began to pound inside his chest. He knew he was in big, big trouble.

Proud Penguin tried to remember everything his parents had taught him to do if he was being chased by killer whales, but his mind went blank. The only thing he could think to do was to try to hide in the middle of the school of squid and hope the whales wouldn't be able to find him. So that's what he did.

But as soon as the whales arrived, the squid scattered in many different directions and Proud Penguin wasn't hidden anymore. In a panic, he dove down as deep as he could and searched for another place to hide. He'd been holding his breath for ten minutes already and knew he could only stay down deep for another ten. It wasn't enough time. The killer whales would be waiting for him. They got closer and closer. He had to get to the safety of the shore. He had to get out of the water. But how?

Proud Penguin knew he couldn't make it alone. He knew he needed help. But he'd made a very bad choice going off by himself, something he'd been warned all his life not to do. His wings hurt and his lungs hurt and he was just about to give up when something changed.

All of a sudden a huge swarm of penguins surrounded him. His friends darted back and forth and in and out as one giant mass. Proud Penguin's heart swelled with relief and joy. Together, the large group of penguins raced toward the shore. Confused, the killer whales lost sight of their prey for a moment, and it was just enough time for the penguins to get to safety.

When they reached the shore, there was no clapping and whistling and cheering for Proud Penguin. Instead, the adult and baby penguins shook their heads and murmured to one another about the terrible thing Proud Penguin had done. Ashamed and exhausted, Proud Penguin hung his head down and sat down to catch his breath. It wasn't long before his parents found him. He knew what they were going to say before they ever opened their mouths. "I know what I did was wrong," Proud Penguin said. "I am very, very sorry. And I can promise you, I will never, ever, ever go hunting alone again."

His parents accepted his apology and gave him a hug. "We're happy you are safe now, but you have set a terrible example for the young penguins.

When you're ready, we think you need to stand up in front of all the young penguins and explain what you did and what almost happened because of it."

Proud Penguin nodded. "I will."

His parents continued. "And you put all of your friend's lives at risk, too. We think you owe them an apology, as well."

Proud Penguin glanced over at his group of friends and his heart swelled with appreciation. They had saved his life. He took a deep breath and waddled over to tell them how grateful he was and how sorry he was that he'd put them in danger. He hoped they would forgive him.

Chapter Five

Can You Keep a Secret?

HAVE YOU EVER HAD a secret? Has someone ever told you a secret? Is it good or bad to keep secrets? Some secrets are good. For example, if you know that your parents bought a super cool present for your brother or sister and they want it to be a surprise. It would be good to keep that kind of secret, right? But what if someone tells you about something bad? Should you keep it a secret if you know someone is hurting someone, or if someone has stolen something, or if someone is cheating? Is it good to keep those kinds of secrets? No, that's not okay to do.

Peppy Penguin and her friends usually didn't keep any secrets from each other. She liked to tell her close friends everything. But one of her friends wasn't good at keeping secrets. Pesky Penguin often asked way too many questions and then she would go blabbing about everything she found out to everyone she came in contact with. Pesky Penguin was a busybody. So Peppy Penguin learned to be careful not to tell any important secrets to Pesky Penguin. Especially not one as important as the one she had at the moment.

Ever since Peppy Penguin had stayed with her father when he was taking such good care of the baby egg, she had wanted to do something to show her appreciation for her papa and for all the penguin fathers. A week earlier she got a big idea. She would get her friends to help her throw a special surprise party for all the Emperor Penguin Daddys.

But she needed her friends to help her plan what kind of fun things to do and what to eat and how to make all the arrangements so that her papa and all the other daddy penguins would have a big surprise. She would need the help of the mommy penguins.

Peppy Penguin wasn't sure she could trust the itty bitty gray furry penguins to keep the party a secret, so she didn't really want to tell them about it. But she did want them to have a special part in the party. So she thought and thought about how she could include them in the special event that she was planning. She got the idea to write a song titled "Thank You Daddy" for them to whistle. She asked her friends Peppy Penguin and Prudent Penguin to take the itty bitty penguins to a place far from the grown-up penguins every morning so they could teach them the song.

Three days before the party, the furry gray penguins giggled with excitement as they followed the older penguins to a special spot behind a large nunutak that would keep them hidden from the adults. Peppy Penguin had a big smile on her face as she watched the itty bittys disappear across the white ice. So far, they'd been very good about keeping the party a secret. She hoped they could hold on for three more days.

Peppy Penguin turned to go back towards the shore and before she could get away, Pesky Penguin stood beside her. "Where in the world are all the itty bittys going?" she asked. "And what have you been up to lately? I've seen you talking quietly to all the young penguins. What's going on? Tell me!"

Peppy Penguin sighed. She'd been avoiding Pesky Penguin for days so that she wouldn't have to tell her about the party. She knew how hard it was for Pesky Penguin to keep secrets. But there was no way she could not tell her now without hurting her feelings. So she decided to take the chance and go ahead and tell her about the party. "But please," she begged. "Please don't tell any of the father penguins about it. I want it to be a big surprise."

"Oh, I won't tell anyone. I promise," said Pesky Penguin. "What can I do to help?"

Peppy Penguin thought for a second. "Can you help the group that's fishing for krill?" she asked, pointing toward the half dozen friends who were getting ready to dive into the water. "We're trying to get enough food so that none of our fathers will have to go hunting for a whole day."

"Sure. No problem," said Pesky Penguin. She slid off on the ice toward the shore to meet the others.

As Peppy Penguin watched her go, she thought maybe she'd been wrong about her friend. Maybe Pesky Penguin really could keep a secret after all.

Or not.

One day before the party, when Peppy Penguin was making all the last minute arrangements, her papa approached her. "What are you up to, little one?"

"Nothing much, Papa," she said.

"How's the party coming along?" he asked with a big grin on his face.

Peppy Penguin froze in place. "What party? What are you talking about?"

Her father chuckled. "A little bird told me that you've been planning a big party for all the fathers. Is it true?"

Peppy penguin scowled. "Was the little bird who told you named Pesky Penguin by any chance?"

Her father lowered his voice. "Don't be angry with her, little one. She didn't mean to tell me. It happened by accident."

Peppy Penguin was furious. "I never should have told her! I knew she couldn't keep a secret."

Peppy Penguin's eyes filled with tears. "Now she's ruined everything."

Her father reached out his wing and brushed it across her face and wiped away her tears. "I'm sorry, little one. But everything is not ruined. You will still throw a wonderful party tomorrow. And I'm the only father who knows about it, so it'll still be a big surprise."

Peppy Penguin perked up a bit, as she wiped the tears from her eyes. "Are you sure you're the only one who knows about the party?" she asked.

"I'm pretty certain. I had a serious heart to heart talk with Pesky Penguin about the importance of keeping things quiet. We also talked about the difference between when we should keep quiet and when we need to tell our parents about things."

"Do you think she really understood?" asked Peppy Penguin.

"I think she did."

"Well, I sure hope so. I guess we'll find out tomorrow."

And thankfully, when all the young penguins gathered their fathers together and the itty bitty penguins whistled their special song, the fathers seemed truly surprised. All except one.

Peppy Penguin's father winked and smiled at her. The party turned out to be loads of fun for everyone. They ate tons of food and the daddy penguins were so happy that they could relax and not have to hunt that day. Then many of the young penguins gave special gifts to their fathers to let them know how much they appreciated them.

As Peppy Penguin was watching everyone with great satisfaction, Pesky Penguin approached her. "I'm really sorry that I told your dad about the secret. He was not happy with me for spoiling the surprise and we had a long talk about the importance of others being able to trust one another. I'm sure you are very disappointed, but I hope you can forgive me and give me another chance to gain your trust back"

Peppy Penguin stood up and hugged her friend. "I was very sad when I found out that you told my dad, but we too had a good talk and he helped me realize that we need to forgive our friends. So yes I forgive you."

At the end of the day, all the Emperor Penguin families left the party with their wings wrapped around each other and wide smiles on their happy faces.

Chapter Six

The Day We Welcomed Others

ALL THE YOUNG PENGUINS had been getting along great all through the bright sunny days of summer. Laughter rang through the air as they swam and played on the ice and filled their bellies day after day. It had been the best and longest summer ever. But one day towards the end of the summer season and before winter arrived, everything changed.

Peppy Penguin and a dozen of her friends relaxed on the shore after having spent most of the morning diving deep for krill. They rested quite far from the rest of the penguins in their favorite isolated spot. Most of the penguins had their eyes closed, but Prudent Penguin kept on the lookout for danger. She was the first to see the strangers pop up out of the water.

One by one, a group of about a hundred penguins slid up onto the icy shore. They looked like Emperor Penguins, but something was very different about them. Their black was not quite black, their white was not quite white, and their yellow stripe was pale almost to the point of being invisible. And they talked funny.

"Goooooood moooorning!" they said, bobbing their heads up and down.

Peppy Penguin and her friends stared at the newcomers, then looked at each other. All of them were wide awake now. No one spoke, but they all had many thoughts streaming through their minds. Who were these strangers and where did they come from? Why were there so many of them? What did they want?

Peppy Penguin stepped forward and spoke with a voice full of suspicion. "Who are you and where are you from?"

The large group of penguins didn't respond. Some cocked their heads to one side and whispered amongst themselves. Others just blinked and nodded and looked around.

Peppy Penguin spoke up again in a louder voice. "WHO ARE YOU? WHAT DO YOU WANT?"

The newcomers continued to talk amongst themselves, but they still didn't answer the questions. Peppy Penguin and her friends didn't know what to do, so they gathered into a huddle to talk about the situation. They'd never met strangers before. None of them were sure what to do.

"Do you think one of us should hurry back to talk to our parents about this?" asked Prudent Penguin. They all nodded in agreement. Prudent Penguin broke out of the huddle and hurried across the ice in the direction of the rest of the flock. The rest kept peeking over their shoulders at the large crowd of strangers. The newcomers stared back at them.

"Do you think they're dangerous?" asked Practical Penguin.

Peaceable Penguin shook her head. "I don't think so. They seem friendly enough."

"But why can't they talk to us?" asked Pesky Penguin. "What's wrong with them?"

No one knew the answer to that. Some of the friends were nervous, so they decided to stay in their huddle and wait for Prudent Penguin to return with their parents.

It seemed like forever before they saw a few black and white spots moving toward them from across the ice. The young penguins glanced at the strangers. They all seemed a bit nervous as they watched the grown-up penguins get closer and closer.

Peppy Penguin recognized her mother and father and a couple of the other older ones from the flock. When they arrived at the shore, all the young penguins scurried behind them as the adults approached the crowd of newcomers. They strained their ears to hear what was being said. Peppy Penguin was surprised to see that her mother was doing most of the talking.

After a few minutes, the newcomers seemed to relax and laugh a bit. Peppy Penguin waited with eagerness to find out what they were talking about. She didn't have to wait long. Her mother waved her over.

Peppy Penguin stood at her mother's side and listened as her mother explained something in a strange language. When she finished, she turned to Peppy Penguin. "These are Emperor Penguins from the far west side of the continent," she said. "Their hunting grounds ran out of fish, so they've made a very long journey to try to find a better source of food. We've invited them to stay here with us."

Peppy Penguin frowned. "But if they come eat our food, there won't be enough for us to eat!"

"There's plenty of food for everyone," her mother said with a stern look on her face. "You mustn't think like that."

Peppy Penguin still didn't understand why the strange looking penguins who talked funny had to come to their side of the continent. "Can't they go somewhere else?" she asked.

"Oh dear." Her mother sighed and put a wing to her mouth. "How about you go gather all your friends and your father and I will come and explain everything."

So Peppy Penguin did what her mother asked her to do. When they'd all huddled into a circle, her parents began to speak. They explained about being friendly and kind to strangers. "Just because other penguins don't look exactly like you or talk like you, they are all still part of our penguin family. And families take care of one another, right?"

Some of the young penguins nodded, others scrunched up their faces and frowned. Pesky Penguin spoke up first. "So you're saying we need to make friends with them?"

"That's exactly what we're saying," said Peppy Penguin's father.

The young penguins looked at each other. "But we don't speak their language," said Practical Penguin.

"It doesn't matter. They are family. We are all related. Just be friendly and smile," said Peppy Penguin's mother. "Everyone smiles in the same language."

So the group of young penguins broke out of their huddle and even though they were a bit nervous, they waddled over to greet the newcomers. Big smiles were exchanged, along with a few words that weren't well understood. But it didn't matter. The penguins all started to laugh and play and that day marked the beginning of new friendships that lasted for many, many years. The penguin family grew larger and stronger because they decided to be kind and because they showed a welcoming, friendly attitude.

AFTERWORD

Thanks again for picking up this book! You are participating in making our world a better place.

For more of our Karma for Kids books please visit us at:
www.karmaforkidsbooks.wordpress.com
or
www.findyourwaypublishing.com

Find Norma MacDonald and her books online at Amazon.com.

Ethan the Eagle and Friends; Short Stories, Fuzzy Animals, and Life Lessons by Norma MacDonald

Billy Brown Bear and Friends; Short Stories, Fuzzy Animals, and Life Lessons by Norma MacDonald

Humble Heron and Friends; Short Stories, Fuzzy Animals, and Life Lessons by Norma MacDonald

Peter Penguin and Friends; Short Stories, Fuzzy Animals, and Life Lessons by Norma MacDonald

Lucy Llama and Friends; Short Stories, Fuzzy Animals, and Life Lessons by Norma MacDonald

Other books that we recommend to help children learn important life lessons:

Guaranteed Success for Kindergarten; 50 Easy Things You Can Do Today! by Marrae Kimball

Guaranteed Success for Grade School; 50 Easy Things You Can Do Today! by Marrae Kimball

The Secret Combination to Middle School: Real Advice from Real Kids, Ideas for Success, and Much More! by Marrae Kimball

NORMA MACDONALD

If you have ideas for stories, please feel free to share and send them to:

Melissa Eshleman
Find Your Way Publishing, Inc.
PO Box 667
Norway, ME 04268
Melissa@findyourwaypublishing.com

www.findyourwaypublishing.com

Thank you!

www.ingramcontent.com/pod-product-compliance
Lightning Source LLC
Chambersburg PA
CBHW071345130626
46556CB00005B/2036